When the Bees Fly Home

Andrea Cheng • Illustrations by Joline McFadden

TILBURY HOUSE, PUBLISHERS • GARDINER, MAINE

To Nathaniel, enjoy!

jmcfadden

The beeswax is smooth. I pass it from hand to hand until it is soft enough to mold.
Then I form the shimmering wings of a honey bee.

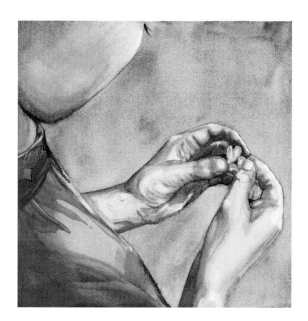

In flight, a bee's two pairs of wings move 180 times per second, but it only flies at about 15 miles per hour. A dragonfly can fly twice as fast.

Dad calls me. "Jonathan, come and unload these supers." So I set my bee down gently in a corner of the truck and jump to the ground.

Dad is silent as he works. The muscles in his arms bulge and shine with sweat. His face strains with the weight of the supers and the stress of this dry spell.

Suddenly I drop a super on my toe and cringe as I wait for the pain to hit.

   "Get back in the truck," Dad orders. I go but still I hear him mutter.

He says I might as well stay home. I am no help at all.

As I inspect my swollen toe, I know Dad is right. My arms are so skinny—even my four-year-old brother is stronger. He likes to say that he is a beekeeper like Dad. He goes around the house wearing a sheet like a bee veil and pretending to smoke the hives. Not me. I just want the wax.

Dad heads off toward the hives without even a word to me. I think at first of following him to see the honey bees come and go as they fly around the hive. I like to watch them, and sometimes I see them do their dance. But my toe is throbbing. I stay in the truck and form the thick body and tiny legs of my wax bee.

Scout bees do a special "waggle" dance to give the other workers directions to where there are flowers with lots of nectar. They dance faster if there is so much nectar that they need more bees to bring it in.

When Dad comes back he is mad because he got stung under his eye. But I think he feels bad about my toe because he tosses me a big glob of fresh wax for the ride home and offers me a drink of ice tea from the thermos.

Dad says that the dry spell has gone on so long that the honey will be slim this year. The clover blossoms are small and few. The locust flowers are wilting in the sun. That means less money than the little we already have. We pass the ice cream store and I hope for a second that Dad will stop because of my toe, but instead he speeds up.

Each hive has one queen bee who lays about 1,500 eggs per day; thousands of female worker bees who do all the work and guard the hive, and several hundred male bees called drones, who live in the hive until they are needed to mate with a new queen from another hive.

When we pull in, Mom is working in the garden. My brother Nicholas runs to the truck and I see Dad smile like he never does at me as he picks up his sturdy son. Mom knits her brow when she sees me hop.

"What happened?" she asks.

"Dropped a super on my toe," I say, sitting down in the grass.

During the honey-gathering season there are 40,000 to 60,000 bees in a beehive. Worker bees live for about 35 days. They do not sleep, but sometimes they will rest in an empty cell.

Mom gets ice wrapped in two checkered towels to hold on my toe, then she waits to see what I have made today. She picks up the bee carefully and turns it around in her hand.

"Perfect," she says. I know she will put it on the shelf by her bed with the other tiny wax animals—a cow with its calf, a pair of geese. I know she looks forward to each new addition.

For a hive to make two pounds of honey on a good day, its worker bees will fly 110,000 miles and bring back nectar from 4 million flowers. Each bee can carry half her body weight in pollen and nectar.

As bees gather nectar and pollen, they brush the pollen against the female part of a plant so that it produces seeds—or fruit or vegetables or grains. Much of the food that we eat grew because it was pollinated by bees.

Mom looks over at Dad. "How was the day?"

Dad doesn't answer, so I do. "The same," I say.

She points to the drooping parsley. "I watered this morning and look."

I nod.

Only Nicholas doesn't seem to care about the dry spell. He shows Dad how strong he is getting. Dad feels his muscle and says yes, it really is very big.

That night my toe throbs and I cannot sleep. I think about the bees. They are getting sluggish. Their dances are slow. Only Dad works in a frenzy. I get up and hop into the kitchen to get more ice.

The first common honey bees in North America were brought by the Pilgrims to pollinate their apple trees. Native Americans called these honey bees the "White Man's Fly."

There is Mom at the stove.

"What are you doing?" I ask.

"Making candles," she says. The smell is sweet like the wax I always mold in my hands. "Tomorrow is the farmer's market. I will try to sell a few." She pours the wax into small square molds. When it hardens, I take them out and set them in a line on the table. Ordinary candles. I make a tiny chick with a drip of wax. Suddenly I have an idea.

Bees bring nectar back to the hive in their special "honey stomachs" and give it to house bees in the hive, who store it in empty cells. Enzymes from the bees and evaporation concentrate the nectar into honey.

"How about I decorate your candles?" I say. I make a family of tiny wax ducks and press it onto the top of a candle. Then I form a few small honey bees and arrange them around the side of a candle. I make the candle into their home.

"The bees are flying into the hive to avoid the rain," I tell Mom.

Mom strokes my skinny arm. She adjusts the ice on my toe. "Better?"

I nod.

Worker bees build honeycomb with wax they secrete from their abdomens. They build hexagonal cells to store honey or pollen and to house their baby bees, and peanut-shaped cells to hold infant queen bees.

By morning the table is covered with our animal candles. Dad gets up before the sun and looks over our work. He picks up the candle with the bees.

"Do you think we could save this one?" he asks.

"What for?" I ask.

"For me," he says, putting it on the windowsill. Then he looks more closely at how I have arranged the bees near the entrance of the hive. Together we look out the kitchen window. The sun is rising between thick gray clouds. The air is heavy.

"Your bees may know something we don't," he says.

Bees cluster around the queen in the hive during a cold winter, eating honey, vibrating, and trading places to keep warm. To cool the hive in hot weather they bring water into the hive and evaporate it by fanning their wings.

Our candles sell fast. By ten o'clock there are no more. Our coffee can is full of money. A lady stops at our empty table. "Got any more?" she asks.

I shake my head.

"All sold out," says Mom.

"Can I place an order then? What I'd like is a snail candle."

I write that down and tell her I'll have it next week. By noon we have more than forty new orders.

When Dad comes home, we show him our heavy coffee can and my order sheet. He can hardly believe it. He stays up late with me and Mom as we work on our next batch of candles.

"Amazing," he says as I form the antennae of a snail and then stick it on the candle. Dad lights the wick of his bee candle.

"The bees were flying home all day today, Jonathan," he says.

Wild bees will make their home in a hollow tree or between the walls of a building. The modern hive box is designed so that we can remove the honey without killing the bees or destroying their home.

This time we make even more candles—with turtles and frogs and doves. Dad holds the extra wax in his hands so it will be warm and easier to mold. Suddenly we hear a sound like tapping on the window. I look at Dad. He picks up the bee candle and the three of us go out to the front porch. The raindrops are big and far apart at first, but in a few minutes it is pouring.

"I'm going in," Mom says. "Just like the bees, I go in when it rains."

Each bee colony has its own distinct odor, and its bees can recognize hive members or robber bees by smell. When a worker bee stings, she dies afterwards because her sting has barbs and she can't pull it out without tearing her abdomen.

We hear the screen door slam. Then a gust of wind blows out the candle, but Dad and I are not ready to go in yet. We walk into the darkness of our front yard.

"Your bees were right," Dad says. Then we just stand there with our arms touching, feeling the water run down.

The survival of a bee colony depends upon thousands and thousands of bees working together, each one doing its job.

TILBURY HOUSE, PUBLISHERS
2 Mechanic Street • Gardiner, ME 04345
800–582-1899 • www.tilburyhouse.com

First Printing: May 2001 • 10 9 8 7 6 5 4 3 2 1

• To my brother, the bee man. —A. C.

Library of Congress Cataloging-in-Publication Data
Cheng, Andrea.
When the bees fly home / Andrea Cheng ; illustrated by Joline McFadden.
p. cm.
Summary: The son of a beekeeper, Jonathan is not sturdy enough to do some of the work, but with the support of his mother he finds a way to help the family and form a bond with his father. Includes bee facts.
ISBN 0-88448-238-3 (Hardcover : alk. paper)
[1. Beekeepers—Fiction. 2. Bee culture—fiction. 3. Honeybees—Fiction.] I. McFadden, Joline, ill. II. Title.
PZ7.C41943 Wh 2002
[E]—dc21   2002001253

Design by Geraldine Millham, Westport, Massachusetts
Editorial and production by Jennifer Elliott, Audrey Maynard, Barbara Diamond
Color separations by Integrated Composition Systems, Spokane, Washington
Printing and binding by Worzalla Publishing, Stevens Point, Wisconsin

BEE RESOURCES

- A companion web site to NOVA's program "Tales from the Hive" is at http://www.pbs.org/wgbh/nova/bees/ It features excellent photography and information.
- The National Honey Board Web Site at http://www.honey.com features history, facts, recipes, games, and a teacher's guide.
- *Bee Culture,* the leading bee magazine in the beekeeping industry, featuring over five years of archived articles, contacts, and more, can be seen at http://www.BeeCulture.com.
- The Burleson's Honey Web Site at http://www.burlesons.com/facts-and-figures/honey-/quiz.htm features a quiz to see how much you know about bees and honey.
- A neuroscientist studying bee vision has set up a B-Eye Web Site at http://cvs.anu.edu.au/andy/beye/ beyehome.html where you can see the world through the eyes of a honeybee.
- The Sue Bee Honey Web Site at http://www.suebeehoney.com contains bee facts and honey recipes.